MATT FAULKNER

A Taste of
Colored Water

SIMON & SCHUSTER BOOKS FOR YOUNG READERS
New York   London   Toronto   Sydney

It was Abbey Finch who started it all.

Seems Abbey'd gone on another shopping trip to the
big city with her mama and she'd seen a sign, clear as
day, hanging over a water bubbler that read COLORED. We
thought she was crazy. Who'd ever heard of "colored" water
coming out of a bubbler?

More 'n likely this was just another one of her stories. Everyone knew Abbey was a first-rate fibber. But good heavens—colored water! What if it were true? And crazy or not, Abbey made it sound so fine! That girl sure could talk.

Jelly (that's short for Julius) was my cousin and best friend. He and I pondered the wondrous possibilities of colored water all the way home. The more we talked, the more we wanted to see it and taste it!

Jelly said, "LuLu,"—that's my name, short for Lucresia—"we got to get a look at that bubbler. Abbey might be crazy, but we'd be even crazier if we didn't see for ourselves."

I, of course, agreed.

We just had to find a way to get to the big city, that's all. Didn't matter that neither Jelly nor I had ever been there. That wasn't important. We'd made a vow, y'see, and the wheels of fate were turning.

And wouldn't you know it, the wheels of fate rolled right up onto Jelly's front lawn the next morning. It verged on the miraculous, and this is how it happened—Uncle Jack borrowed a tractor and the tired old thing broke down. Jelly and I were sitting on the front porch the very moment Uncle Jack decided to drive into the big city to get a new part for the tractor's engine.

We offered to come along and keep him company. Uncle Jack
wouldn't have it, though.

"Don't test me now, children. I'm busy."

Jelly and I were nothing if not persistent. We pestered poor ol' Uncle
Jack till he gave in.

"Enough!" he said. "But I don't want no silliness from y'all and I'll
expect you to stay in the truck while I'm in the store. Understand?"

"Oh, yessuh!" said Jelly, as we climbed into the truck.

There we were, side by side by side in Uncle Jack's truck, bouncing along on that road to the big city. Life was good! We had a jug of lemonade and some peaches, too, and it was such fun going on about the colored water, whispering and giggling. Uncle Jack had no idea. That was a good thing 'cause he woulda turned the truck right around if he'd known what we were up to.

The big city wasn't like home. No, not at all. We watched the buildings along the road grow bigger and bigger. There were hardly any trees and no fields, but lots, lots more people, walking and talking, or just sitting around fanning themselves in the heat.

"Mind yourselves, now," said Uncle Jack. "No more silliness."

The big city made me nervous. And I knew Jelly
was nervous 'cause he was holding my hand so tight.
I think Uncle Jack was nervous too.

After what seemed like forever, Uncle Jack gave a big sigh. "There it is—city hall. The tractor shop is just across the street."

I looked at Jelly, and Jelly looked at me—city hall! We made it! Colored water was so close. Oh, I could taste it already—cherry, lemon, orange, and apple—all those flavors in one gulp! Jelly and I were looking all about, but there was no sign of a bubbler. What if Abbey had just been telling another fib?

Uncle Jack brought the truck to a stop and put his big hand on
Jelly's shoulder. "Stay in the truck while I go in the store. I won't be
but a minute." He stepped out of the truck and slammed the door.
"Stay put!"

As soon as Uncle Jack walked in the store, we hopped out of
the truck. "Look, LuLu!" cried Jelly. He pointed across the street.
Sitting close by the big white city hall was a water bubbler, and
hanging above it was a sign that said COLORED.

"Let's go!" I hollered.

We ran across the street. I looked
up the hill and saw the bubbler again.
There it was, just waiting for us.

"Let's race!" said Jelly, and we rushed up the hill. Jelly was faster than me and sprinted ahead. I caught up to him at the top of the little hill, and we stood there, staring at the bubbler.

I told Jelly to go ahead and have a drink. He'd gotten to the bubbler first; it was only fair.

"Naw," he said. "You go first. Ladies before gentlemen." Jelly just stood there smiling. "I'll stand back here and keep an eye out for Daddy. You go ahead and have a drink."

It was such a kind thing for him to do. So I curtsied and took a step toward the bubbler.

Funny, it didn't look any different than a regular water bubbler. I had thought it might look special, sort of heavenly, but it looked as plain as can be.

I stepped up onto the stone, grabbed the handle, gave it a twist, and watched as the colored water bubbled up. It sparkled in the sun and was so pretty.

Just then I heard singing. Down the other side of the hill, I saw a crowd of folks marching along the road. They carried signs and they were singing. The singing was so loud, almost like shouting, but they seemed so happy that I wanted to run down and join them. On the other side of the square I could see a whole bunch of policemen and firemen.

They looked as if they were waiting for the marching singers and
I thought maybe they'd all sing a song when they came together.
But that wasn't what happened.

As the parade came closer, I saw the firemen raise their fire hoses and shoot great gushes of water straight into the marching singers. It was a hot day and I thought maybe they were trying to give the marchers a treat, but the water came out so fast and hard it knocked folks clean off their feet. They kept shooting that water, hurting people. I tried to shout— Stop! Stop!—but my throat was so dry, and I started to feel dizzy, like a nest of hot bees was swarming in my head.

Just then I felt Jelly tug at my sleeve. "Whatcha doing?" he said. "You gonna have a drink or not?"

I didn't answer him, just stepped back off the stone and fell down on the ground. Jelly knelt beside me. "Are you all right, LuLu?"

I nodded and told him to hurry up and take his drink of the colored water.

He hopped up on the stone, twisted the handle,
and leaned forward to have a taste.

I didn't even see the policeman at first.

"Get away from there, boy! That water ain't for you. It's for coloreds!" He yanked Jelly down from the bubbler and pushed him to the ground next to me. "Can't you see what's going on?" he shouted. "This is no place for children. Now git!" He yanked the leash and dragged his dog all the way down the hill toward the parade. It snapped and snarled the whole way.

I heard someone calling our names.

"Jelly! LuLu!" It was Uncle Jack.

We raced down the hill.

Uncle Jack met us on the road and carried us back to the truck.
I was so happy to feel his scratchy old beard on my face.

"I told you to stay put!" Uncle Jack yelled. He scolded us pretty fierce. I'd never seen him so angry. Jelly was crying. I soon took to crying too. "Aw, now, I'm sorry," said Uncle Jack. "I was jus' angry 'cause y'all scared me."

I was so tired, I could barely keep my eyes open. The humming of the tires was making me so sleepy. I must have slept all the way home, but before I nodded off, I do remember wondering about the marching singers and the firemen and the policeman's dog, and, last of all, I remember Jelly asking—

"Daddy, what color does a person have to be to get a taste of colored water?"

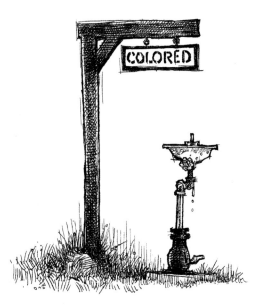

AFTERWORD

————✦————

"What color does a person have to be?"

Less than ten years after the Civil War ended, a series of unfair laws (commonly referred to as "Jim Crow" laws) were enacted in the southern and border states of the U.S. The main goal of these laws was to suppress and demean the black-skinned American population, the former slaves, and to keep them separate from the white-skinned Americans, those who once benefitted from the institution of slavery. "Separate but equal" was the catchphrase of these laws. But while blacks were forced to attend separate schools, ride in separate sections of public transportation, and sit in separate areas of restaurants and movie theaters, etc., these separate facilities and accommodations were more often than not far inferior to those set aside for whites. This is why a sign labeled COLORED could be hung above a water bubbler in a southern town. It was placed there to indicate a less than adequate water fountain at which only black Americans should drink. It wasn't until the 1950s and 1960s, a time called the civil rights era, that these laws were challenged and, with great struggle, abolished.

I grew up in a northern town where there were no water fountains with the word COLORED hanging over them. When I was a boy it would've surprised me to learn that the word COLORED hung over a water fountain didn't mean that this was a magical place where fruit-flavored water flowed on demand. I know that I would've been very troubled to learn that COLORED hung over a water fountain actually meant: "This run-down, piece-of-junk, bad-tasting water fountain is for people with colored or black skin and this is because black people are worth less than lighter-skinned, white people." Being small and full of questions about what was fair and what wasn't, I would've wanted to know just what it was about black people that made them "worth less" in the eyes of white-skinned grown-ups. "What did the black people do wrong?" I would've asked. "Is there something about their black skin that makes them bad?"

As I grew older and less likely to ask difficult questions, I learned by the words and actions of many of the white grown-ups in my northern town that while black didn't necessarily mean "worth less," it did mean other things just as unfair. I was taught that black meant living in the poorest part of the city. Black meant being hungry and going to run-down schools. To many of the grown-ups in my northern town, black especially meant ignorance, anger, and violence. Black was something to fear. And, most importantly, it was quietly made clear to me that black was something that I should be very happy that I was not.

Of all the odd lessons I learned about black and white, the one I found most confusing was learning that being black didn't always mean bad things. I wondered how this could be when I'd learned so much that was bad and fearful about being black. I was assured, however, that there were some very special black people. Movie stars, politicians and community leaders, athletes, musicians, comedians, and even engineers and scientists. These were the good, beautiful, and talented black people. But they were different—not like the rest. *How could this be,* I wondered? Good, bad, angry, talented, violent, or special—every day I saw these very same qualities in all the white people in my northern town. In time I made up my mind that being good or bad didn't have anything to do with having black or white skin.

It's been many years since I lived in that northern town and yet I still don't fully understand why the grown-ups taught me all those crazy things about black and white skin. But as I look back, I realize that these strange lessons weren't about skin color at all. What I believe I was being taught was the lesson of fear. They were teaching me that life is something to be afraid of, and if I can just make someone else feel that they are worth less than me, feel frightened of me, then somehow this would make things better for me. By taking someone else down I could build myself up. That, simply, is not true.

I've done my best to unlearn all those rules about black and white and yet sometimes I still make mistakes. This makes me sad, but I've learned to just keep on trying. And I've learned, too, that as difficult as it might be, asking scary questions about unfair rules could be the best thing that a young person can do for the grown-ups in her or his life.

It's my wish that we take strength from the courageous ones who came before us and learn to question oppression, racism, segregation—and all forms of intolerance—and begin to promote compassion for all.

Matt Faulkner, San Francisco Bay, California, 2007

＊＊＊

This book is dedicated to all the Dreamers (you know who you are)!
I believe it's time to wake the nation.
—M. F.

"I have freed many slaves,
and could have freed thousands more if they only knew they were slaves."
—Harriet Tubman, 1820-1913

SIMON & SCHUSTER BOOKS FOR YOUNG READERS
An imprint of Simon & Schuster Children's Publishing Division ˜ 1230 Avenue of the Americas, New York, New York 10020
Copyright © 2008 by Matt Faulkner
All rights reserved, including the right of reproduction in whole or in part in any form.
SIMON & SCHUSTER BOOKS FOR YOUNG READERS is a trademark of Simon & Schuster, Inc.
Book design by Jessica Sonkin ˜ The text for this book is set in Regula Antiqua.
The illustrations for this book are rendered in watercolor and pen and ink.
Manufactured in the United States of America
2 4 6 8 10 9 7 5 3 1
CIP data for this book is available from the Library of Congress.
ISBN-13: 978-1-4169-1629-1 ˜ ISBN-10: 1-4169-1629-6

first
edition